Millicent
and
The Wind

Millicent
and
The Wind

by Robert Munsch
illustrated by Suzanne Duranceau

annick press
toronto • new york • vancouver

Twenty-fourth printing, September 2014

Annick Press Ltd.

We acknowledge the support of the Canada Council for the Arts, the Ontario Arts Council, and the Government of Canada through the Canada Book Fund (CBF) for our publishing activities.

ONTARIO ARTS COUNCIL
CONSEIL DES ARTS DE L'ONTARIO
an Ontario government agency
un organisme du gouvernement de l'Ontario

Cataloging in Publication Data
Munsch, Robert N., 1945-
    Millicent and the wind

(Munsch for kids)
ISBN 0-920236-98-7 (bound) — 0-920236-93-6 (pbk.)

I. Duranceau, Suzanne. II. title   III. series:
Munsch, Robert N., 1945- . Munsch for kids.

PS8576.U58M54 1984   jC813'.54   C84-098923-7
PZ7.M86Mi 1984

Distributed in Canada by:
Firefly Books Ltd.
50 Staples Avenue, Unit 1
Richmond Hill, ON
L4B 0A7

Published in the U.S.A. by Annick Press (U.S.) Ltd.
Distributed in the U.S.A. by:
Firefly Books (U.S.) Inc.
P.O. Box 1338
Ellicott Station, Buffalo, NY 14205

Printed and bound in China

visit us at: **www.annickpress.com**
visit Robert Munsch at: **www.robertmunsch.com**

Also available in e-book format. Please visit **www.annickpress.com/ebooks**
for more details. Or scan

To Alma
and Julia

One morning, when all the world was quiet, Millicent stood on her mountaintop and looked at the world. She saw trees and rocks and sunshine and clouds, but no other children. Far away in the valley was where the other children lived. It took three whole days just to walk there. Millicent had no friends.

On this morning someone whispered very softly, "Hey, Millicent." Millicent looked all around, but all she saw were trees and rocks and sunshine and clouds.

Then someone whispered louder, "Hey, Millicent."

This time Millicent said, "There is nothing I see except trees and rocks and sunshine and clouds, and they cannot talk. Who are you?"

illicent," whispered the voice, "I am the wind."

"Oh, no," said Millicent, "the wind howls and roars and whistles and rustles. It doesn't talk."

Then the wind blew Millicent's dress around her legs, very softly touched her face and hair, and said, "I am the very wind of all the world. I blow when I wish and talk when I want to. The day is so quiet and the sunshine so yellow that I feel like talking right now."

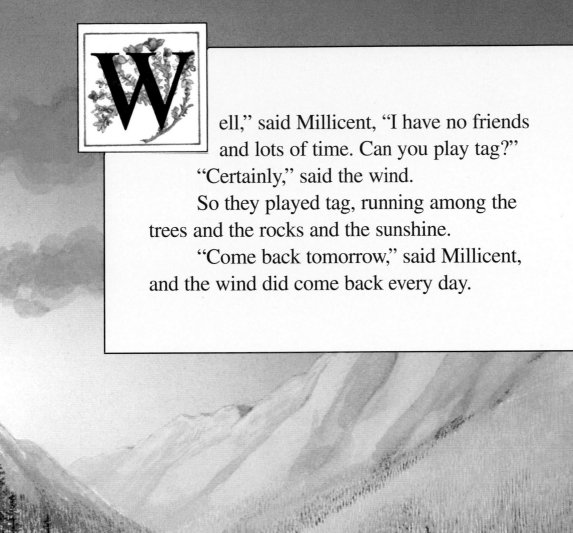

Well," said Millicent, "I have no friends and lots of time. Can you play tag?"

"Certainly," said the wind.

So they played tag, running among the trees and the rocks and the sunshine.

"Come back tomorrow," said Millicent, and the wind did come back every day.

**B**ut there came a time when Millicent was not there. She and her mother had gone down over the rocks and into the deep forest. They were walking all the way to the valley to buy the things they needed. So the wind could not play tag that day. It blew all over the world looking for Millicent, but Millicent was walking far at the bottom of a forest and the wind could not find her.

illicent and her mother walked for three days and finally came to the valley where people lived. When they walked through the valley, all the children came out of their houses and looked at Millicent. One boy with red hair said to Millicent, "Who are you and where do you come from?"

S he said, "My name is Millicent. I live on the mountaintop. I have no friends except the wind." And the red-haired boy said, "The wind is nobody's friend," and all the children started to yell, "Millicent, Millicent, lives on a mountain-top! Go home, Millicent!"

Then a strange thing happened. A very large wind came and picked the red-haired boy right up into the sky and tumbled him around like a leaf until his clothes were all tatters and his hair was a mess.

All the children ran away. Millicent and her mother went to town and bought the things they needed, but Millicent was sorry that the children had run away.

 t took them three whole days to walk back to the mountain. When they got there, Millicent looked at the trees and the rocks and the clouds and the sunshine and wished that she had somebody to play with besides the wind.

ind," said Millicent, "you blow through the hair of every child everywhere in the world. Can you find me someone to play tag with?"

"Boy or girl?" said the wind.

"Get me a friend," said Millicent.

The wind turned into something huge and enormous that rumbled the rocks and bent the trees, and whistled off far away until Millicent could not hear it any more.

But in a little while it came back, and it carried a boy.
The wind put him down.
Millicent looked at the boy. The boy looked at Millicent.

"Let's play," said Millicent, and
they did.

The End

Other books in the Munsch for Kids series:

For information on these titles please visit www.annickpress.com
Many Munsch titles are available in French and/or Spanish, as well as in
board book and e-book editions. Please contact your favorite supplier.